May the incredible
journey of Carol
lift and inspire you.
♡ Cathy

A Beagle Named Carol

Printed in the United States of America

First Printing 2021

ISBN 978-1-7375878-0-4

Dolly Llama® Books
dollyllamabooks.com

Road Dog Media LLC

Illustrations by
Peter Bex

Book Design by
Lauren Wozny

A Beagle Named Carol

by
Cathy Schenkelberg

Illustration by
Peter Bex

Forward

by Meg Moore Burns
Educator, Principal - Sutherland Elementary School Chicago, Illinois

A Beagle Named Carol is an emotional tale of trust, empathy and companionship that feeds the reader's soul. Carol's evolution and bond with her owner is beautifully woven through lyrical text reflective of her Irish roots.

Carol's justified human mistrust transforms her human in healing ways that could not have been anticipated. "Carol's" gift is the melding of two hearts that so desperately needed rescuing and the trust and love embodied in us all. A perfect read for children both big and small.

To all dogs everywhere looking for a forever home, and to the humans whose hearts will be changed forever by their love.

This tale begins in the green hills of County Westmeath,
Set in the midlands of the Republic of Ireland

REPUBLIC OF
IRELAND

DONEGAL
DERRY
ANTRIM
BELFAST
TYRONE
DOWN
FERMANAGH
ARMAGH
MONAGHAN
SLIGO
LEITRIM
MAYO
CAVAN
ROSCOMMON
LONGFORD
LOUTH
WESTMEATH
MEATH
DUBLIN
GALWAY
DUBLIN
GALWAY
OFFALY
KILDARE
LAOIS
WICKLOW
CLARE
CARLOW
KILKENNY
LIMERICK
TIPPERARY
WEXFORD
LIMERICK
WATERFORD
KERRY
WATERFORD
CORK
CORK

N
W E
S

0 1 2 3 4 5 6 7 8 9 10

Once upon a time in County Westmeath
There lived a young beagle quite cheeky yet sweet

A Beagle named Carol
Like a song don't you see

For this Christmas-named Beagle
So longed to be free

Held up in a cage
for some weeks and a year
To be prodded and poked
in a lab

"Oh My Dear!"

This, all for the sake
of science I'm told
This female beagle
locked up in a hold

His name was McGhee
with an 'h' he did spell it

She melted his heart
he knew it, he felt it

McGhee with an 'h'
showed up to this place
To rescue that beagle
with the sweet little face

Carol quietly curled up
not a peep did she make
While the other young beagles
pushed front of the crate

"The one at the back!"
Shouted McGhee with an 'h',
"I want that sweet beagle
I know she is my mate."

At the back of the cage
behind Kringle and Jingle
and dozens of other
Christmas-named beagles

Frightened and skinny
not a peep was no fun
I will nurture and teach her
to dance in the sun

She was shaking so quiet
cuddled up in his arms
It took but a moment
to fall for his charm

But the poor little mite was not willing to eat
Twas love that she needed to get on her feet

Now big brother Ben
came bounding along
To teach her the tunes
for all the dog songs

She learned how to bark
and dig for a bone
She knew in her heart
she was never alone

Sweet Carol-Leena
her confidence grew

Now she was the one
pushing front of the queue

"Tickle my tum"
she all but declares

As she wiggles and jiggles
her legs in the air

This shameless wee pup
no longer afraid

Her light in no bushel
and mischief be made

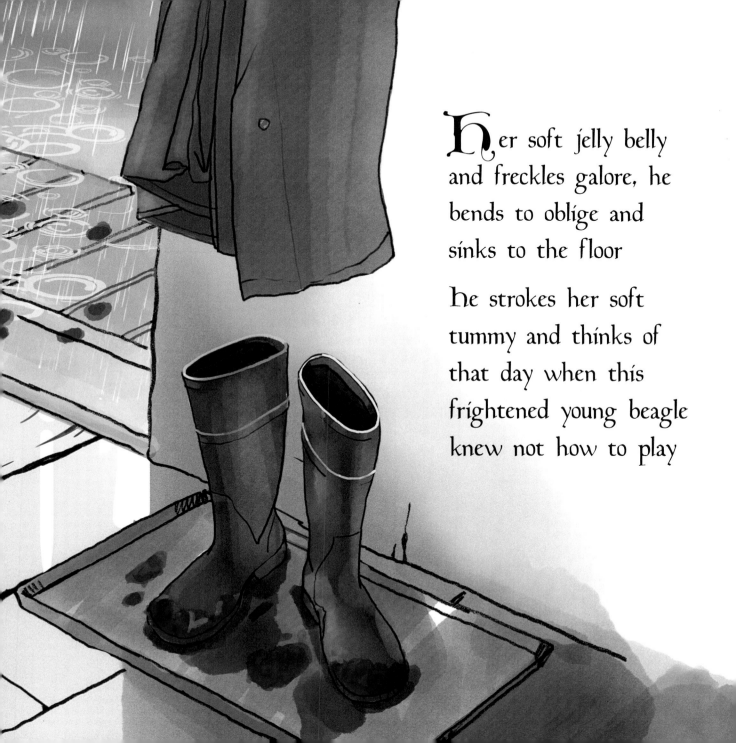

Her soft jelly belly
and freckles galore, he
bends to oblige and
sinks to the floor

he strokes her soft
tummy and thinks of
that day when this
frightened young beagle
knew not how to play

Each day was a challenge
to lessen her fear
for Carol the beagle
cooped up for a year

With sweet brother Ben
to help her be strong
To teach her dog things
As he played along

To run and to fetch
Like all other beagles

To create such a life
That is loved and so regal

His female beagle
so darling and bold

his own precious angel
for all to behold

He painted her nails
They cuddled in bed

A pampered young Carol
so healthy and fed

He took her to work
with Ben by her side

To watch over and guide her
which filled him with pride

Hanging out of the window
hanging out of the car

Both Ben and now Carol
waving off from afar

Now here is a man
a strapping great lad

With an 'h' in his name
like his heart, not half bad

For you see in this story a man saved a dog
But really sweet Carol lifted him from the fog

Dogs save people too
as this story is told

Now McGhee has sweet Carol
still cheeky and bold

Inseparably bonded
now McGhee's little mate

Two hearts found each other
to change both their fate

This book is dedicated
to McGhee with an 'h'
and Carol like a song

So happy together
where indeed they belong